Learn to read with
Baby bug

Words by Sue Graves
Illustrations by Jan Smith

book-studio

Mom gave a present to Baby bug.

"Happy birthday," said Mom. She gave him a hug.

"Wow!" said Baby bug. He dug and he dug.

First he dug up a big green jug.

Next he dug up an old red mug.

Then he dug
up a toy pug.
"Wow!" he
said. "I will
hug this pug."

Just then he
saw a rug.
He gave it
a big tug.

Suddenly out came the rug.

"Where is Baby bug?" said Mom with a shrug.

"Help!"

The end